NOBODIES

Charleston, SC
www.PalmettoPublishing.com

Nobodies
Copyright © 2023 by Rafael Hines

First Edition

Hardcover ISBN: 979-8-8229-2661-5
Paperback ISBN: 979-8-8229-2662-2
eBook ISBN: 979-8-8229-2663-9

NOBODIES

DOMINATION

RAFAEL HINES

WHO ARE THEY?

IT'S A DARK AND STORMY NIGHT, LIKE the beginning of a dramatic horror story. In the middle of a mountainous forest, two humanlike creatures are having a ferocious brawl. It's too dark to identify what exactly is in the midst of this raging struggle, but it's quite clear that they're not human. Growls can be heard. The strength of their paws produces uncanny speed and jumping ability. Their eyes are kindled with rage.

What are they? Where have they come from? What are they fighting for? Let's start at the beginning.

In a secured, secret location lies a large building made for the creation and development of advanced technology. It's called the Command Center. Inside this building is highly classified activity. There are multiple floors both above and below the surface.

In a certain sector of the building are four kids with special collars on their necks, ranging in age between eight and eleven. They are training inside a giant gymnasium along with animal companions to master their special abilities as scientific prototypes. The oldest, Diesel, and his hamster, Torro are doing strength and problem-solving training. Diesel does the heavy moving and lifting as Torro directs him through a maze machine.

Then there is Angel, and her bird, Phoenix. They're practicing sonic vibrations control. Angel trains Phoenix to hone her high-frequency voice by targeting things such as the ground and water to see the result. They also aim at objects such as glass, bricks, or metals to see what frequency will break them with the bird's voice.

Cato and his cat, Lynx, are in an obstacle course with pop-up targets. These test the catlike instincts of the two along with their speed and agility. The targets consist of traps that attack or restrain the duo to put their reflexes to the ultimate trial. With how easily they evade and destroy the targets, it doesn't seem like much of an ordeal.

Last, and also the youngest, are Chaise and his dog, Coyote. They're Cato and Lynx's opponents in the course, coming from the opposite direction. Along with targets to test their canine instincts and reflexes, the two make quick work of their obstacles to meet their feline friends at the midpoint. Their favorite part is to face off with each other there since it challenges them more.

They don't know it yet, but one day these kids and their animal companions are going to save the world.

The children are taught that there's a purpose behind the training. Not all the young ones' parents are present in their lives, so the children report to their primary instructor. The life they're living isn't quite the ideal childhood, but the group is granted a decent amount of supervised free time to be kids.

As five years pass, the character inside each child grows more noticeable. The psychic link with their animal partners become stronger as well.

Diesel is kind and enjoys lifting and problem-solving. His hamster, Torro, is more on the aggressive side. Thankfully the attitudes aren't reversed because Diesel is becoming a big guy, and Chaise antagonizes him. It will be nice to see them fight.

Chaise is the wild, rebellious type. Although the youngest of the crew, he seems to feel the need to prove he's tougher than he looks. He's also territorial, and Coyote is unconditionally loyal to him; he follows Chaise's lead. Because of their duels, Chaise has a level of respect for Cato. That makes the two close friends.

Angel is the most relaxed character of the bunch. She laughs, jokes, and plays with little care in the world. That's possibly because of the overprotective lookout she has in her bird, Phoenix. Phoenix is mostly quiet. Her voice is too dangerous for occasional singing. Thankfully their telepathic link provides them with the ability to communicate, so Phoenix watches, listens, and warns Angel when necessary.

Cato keeps the team together. His wisdom and sense of understanding helps form a medium where they all can tolerate one another's differences such as Chaise's attitude or Diesel's sarcasm. Lynx is Cato's right-hand man. He helps Cato when he can and always watches Cato's back.

Lynx and Coyote have also formed a bond. They both enjoy pouncing on each other, practicing their hunting skills. Chaise and Angel, on the other hand, don't get along. Angel finds Chaise's wild cockiness annoying, and she pranks Chaise often. There's also an intimate bond between Angel and Cato that goes unspoken. This causes Angel and Chaise to respect each other enough for the sake of Cato.

As time and training progresses, the teenagers grow more interested in the outside world. They begin to want to interact with normal kids and try the things they do. The team starts to feel like prisoners. Their inability to engage their interests discourages the team and provokes Chaise to protest for their freedom. Unfortunately, the teenagers' wish cannot be granted, so they continue with their usual everyday schedules.

One day during their free time, Chaise receives an email from an anonymous sender titled, "In Case You Wanted to Be Free." Of course it touches a very sensitive place in his mind. He opens and reads the anonymous message.

The next day during training, Chaise proposes to Cato that they should break out of the facility and take their freedom by force. He says he also knows how to take the restriction collars off. Cato, not taking Chaise's words seriously, responds.

"Yeah! Let's run away with no food or shelter AND worry about being hunted for the rest of our lives. It'll be fun!"

Chaise, demanding respect for his words, reacts by destroying one of Cato's targets as his friend is about to strike it. He stands in place of it and blocks Cato's strike to get his attention.

"I'm serious," Chaise says. "Let's at least run this by Diesel 'n' Angel."

Cato realizes Chaise is passionate about this idea. He responds, "OK, but if they think it's a bad idea, will you let it go?"

Chaise smirks, then continues the training saying, "We'll see."

Later that day during the group's break, they gather, and Chaise brings up the subject. The idea of a breakout seems refreshing to them. They've never thought they could get rid of the collars around their necks, let alone live like normal people. This persuades Angel and Diesel to quickly agree with Chaise's idea.

Surprised, Cato warns the team.

"The outside world can be way more dangerous than this facility we live in. It would probably be best to stay here where we have food and a decent place to sleep. Plus, the punishment for breaking out may be great. We may have to fight for our freedom for the rest of our lives just to avoid finding out how bad the punishment can really be."

Chaise nonchalantly states, "I'll take that risk."

Diesel adds, "People should have the choice to come and go as they please. I'm in."

Angel inserts, "I'd rather try and fail than spend the rest of my life wondering if it were possible. Count me in too."

Cato smiles. He's impressed at the fact that the team finally agrees on something that Chaise has proposed. He submits.

"Cool! It's decided then." He confirms, "We're breakin' out of here...But we need a plan."

ESCAPE

CONSIDERING ALL THE POSSIBLE OUT-comes of the team's escape from the Command Center, Cato warns them about circumstances to watch out for, for example, being tracked down or discovered by civilians. He also gives the team dos and don'ts while in the outside world, such as "always look out for one another" and "never expose our identity."

Afterward, the team puts together a plan to escape. They need certain items and weapons to complete each phase of the plan. After Cato's briefing, the team disperses.

Chaise, while in his room, logs on to his laptop and sends an email to his anonymous source with the subject "Thanks." Before he logs off, he receives a response notice. He clicks on it and reads.

Several nights later, a surveillance camera is scanning a hallway. Suddenly—plink!—an object hits the camera and turns off its feed. The shadows of six figures can be seen running down the hallway. The teens, with their collars off, scurry through the halls of the secret base. Lynx and Coyote trail them.

With Cato and Chaise's aim, they disable all cameras along their exit with throwing darts that they have smuggled before ending their daily training. Eventually alarms go off due to the pattern of video outages. Emergency doors close, and lights shine red.

"Diesel, Torro's up! Plan B!" Cato orders.

Diesel unzips his bag. After using his psychic link to his hamster, Torro crawls out and races toward the closed reinforced emergency doors. The team follows Torro, with Chaise saying, "So much for stealth."

Suddenly Torro transforms into a supersized raging bull as large as a pickup truck, *ramming* the doors open. As Torro keeps charging, Cato orders Angel to tell Phoenix to get ready. She uses her psychic link to her bird, and it takes flight out of her bag. All the kids insert earplugs into their ears and continue their journey. Phoenix flies in front of the teenagers but keeps her distance behind Torro.

Waiting inside the main lobby and front entrance of the building, security points their weapons at the last door. Once the team reaches the front entrance, security yells, "Freeze!" Just at that moment, Torro morphs back into a hamster, and Phoenix flies into the room, screaming. Her supersonic vocals echo throughout the giant room and bring the security to their knees as they yell and hold their ears.

With this given opportunity, Torro takes one last charge. He morphs back into a bull and breaks through the last door with the rest of the team behind him. Angel points at the hearing protection in her ears, teasing the wounded guards, "Special ear pro… from the pros!"

At last, the rogues arrive outside the massive building where Torro shrinks back to a hamster. Diesel picks him up, joking.

"Arms 'n' legs inside the ride at all times." Torro tucks himself inside Diesel's bag on his back.

Phoenix morphs into a giant eagle the size of a personal jet. After they all mount Phoenix, she spreads her enormous wings and lifts into the sky with a single flap. The team celebrates as they escape. They're finally free.

CLOUDY WITH A CHANCE OF RAIN

ABOUT FIVE YEARS AFTER THE CHIL-dren escape the Command Center, in outer space, a colossal space vessel is approaching Earth. Aboard the vessel are various types of creatures dressed in uniform. In the command deck, one of the creatures reports in a foreign language, translating as, "Planet ahead, sir."

The commander responds by nodding. He's covered in a dark cloak, so his face can't be seen. The commander stands about fifteen-feet tall with broad shoulders. He turns toward another and asks, "So, this is your home planet?"

A nervous-looking human standing in front of him replies, "Yes, Lord Draegon."

The commander issues the order, "Prepare for invasion!"

Meanwhile back at the Command Center, a notification pops up on a scientist's monitor. He opens the message and discovers a spacecraft spotted by one of Earth's satellite cameras. The scientist immediately notifies the supervisor.

The supervisor enters and views the screen. Panicking, she quickly grabs a phone and starts a call.

"I know that ship!" she says fearfully as the phone rings.

Over an hour later, a group of black vehicles drives into a forest right outside a small town. Once they get farther into the forest, they come to a stop. A man in a suit exits one of the vehicles and looks around with a beeping device in hand.

As he observes, a voice echoes from within the woods.

"You had tracking devices on us this whole time? What took you so long?"

The man in the suit continues his inspection and answers.

"Thought you all needed some space, so we let you go! But we had to keep tabs on you in case things got out of hand! You understand, right?"

The voice he hears is that of a nineteen year old adult, Cato. He and grown-up Lynx are hiding in a tree. "Yeah, well, things are still intact. What are you doing here now?"

"We're not here to contain you. We're here to ask for your help."

Cato looks confused.

The man in the suit continues.

"There's a big storm coming, and you guys can help bring us some sun."

Cato and Lynx leap out of the tree into the man's view and walk toward him. "A storm, huh? How big we talkin'?" Cato asks.

The man in the suit answers, "We're talking biblical here. The Flood, fire raining from the sky, and a plague of locusts...the fate of the world. Millions will die, and even more can be enslaved as human experiments and such. You and the rest of the Nobodies can stop this. You can be heroes."

Cato and Lynx look at each other as they think of the same thing. Cato signals the rest of his team with a whistle and wave. "Nobodies, huh? That's what you call us?" he says as the rest of the team come out of hiding.

The man in the suit confirms, "It's the name the Command Center gave you. You guys are so top secret that you don't even have identities…for confidentiality purposes, of course."

Cato glances at his team as they join the conversation and echoes, "Nobodies…it fits. I kinda like it."

Chaise steps in, interrupting the conversation.

"Yo, what's goin' on here?" he interrogates. 'N' what do you want, creepy man in black?"

Angel laughs at the nickname Chaise has given the man and adds, "He looks like the dude from *The Matrix*! Mr. Anderson!"

Diesel interrupts, "No, he's the Transporter!"

The Nobodies all laugh together as the man in the suit walks back to his vehicle. He opens the door and insists, "Let's take a ride. I'll explain everything on the way."

"On the way to where?" Chaise grills. "I, kind of, just got back here, and I'd hate to have to relocate over some bull."

The man in the suit returns, "I'll explain that too." Then he enters the vehicle and leaves the door open.

The Nobodies all together lean into a huddle and bicker. Chaise says, "It's a trap. They want us to go without a fight."

Cato argues, "I don't know about that. They knew how to find us the whole time we were gone. That could've been done a long time ago."

Diesel says, "Well, why do they have so many vehicles?"

Chaise answers, "In case we *do* put up a fight!"

Cato says, "Maybe so…but from what the man said, somethin' big is goin' down soon. I don't think we should ignore the chances of that happenin'."

Chaise replies, "Are you crazy? How can you trust somebody so easily?"

Angel says, "We've been out here for a little over five years. Now they wanna show up? At the same time, it's not like they came out with guns or anything. This may be really important, guys."

Diesel says, "Well, we could either go now and fight later…or fight now and end up finding out later. I agree with Angel. They don't seem to wanna take us by force. Maybe we should ask 'em what happens if we say no."

The man sticks his head out of the door.

"I did mention that the fate of the world is at stake, right?" he reminds them.

The team looks at Cato, who counters.

"What if we say no?" he asks.

The man's voice leaves the vehicle.

"World domination!"

The words of the man immobilize the team for a second. Cato finally steps forward and initiates the command.

"Let's go, guys." He walks to the door of the vehicle, stands by to hold it open, and waits for his team.

The Nobodies board the vehicle.

"Tell Phoenix to watch over us from the sky. She needs to alert us as soon as possible if she sees anything suspicious," Cato tells Angel before she enters.

Chaise, being last to enter before Cato, tries to intimidate him by saying, "If this is a setup, I'm kickin' your ass first."

Cato replies with a condescending smile, "You can try."

After everyone is aboard, the convoy begins, and once everyone is comfortable, the man tells his story.

THE ORIGIN

THE MAN IN THE SUIT SAYS, "ABOUT twenty years ago, a group of scientists discovered signs of life on another side of the galaxy. These scientists were members of the Command Center. They assembled a team of explorers, set coordinates, and ventured off in a highly advanced spaceship.

"They traveled for months. Then upon arriving at their destination, the explorers found far more than they expected to. There was another massive spaceship, much greater than the explorers' ship. As they got closer to this spaceship, they realized that their ship was gravitating toward it. The explorers tried to steer away, but the alien spaceship had completely compromised theirs.

"They had no choice but to prepare for what was next. Doors of the alien ship opened and welcomed them in. Once docked, the explorers opened their doors, and these large creatures raided the explorers' ship.

"The aliens were very hostile, yelling in their native language with strange weapons in hand. The aliens gathered all the explorers together and escorted them on board the alien ship. There, they discovered a whole civilization of different types of creatures just living in there.

"The explorers were escorted to a chamber apparently used to hold prisoners. They were used for experiments, studies, and tests day after day. The creatures studied every bit of information they could gather about our species.

"But as the explorers were being studied, they themselves gathered as much info as they could about the aliens and their ship. They discovered that the aliens are really mutated forms of their own natural bodies. The creatures use a type of microchip that seems to have different DNA codes of other creatures on them. The aliens assigned a code to a microchip and implanted it in the brain of its subject. This caused the creature to transform into a combination of an enhanced form of the DNA owner and the subject's own body structure.

"The microchip also seems to compel its subject to follow the commander's orders. It's assumed that the aliens are mostly, if not all, former prisoners of the commander of the ship. The explorers also found their spaceship while they were escorted throughout the ship. It appeared to be intact. This encouraged them to remain hopeful and plan an escape.

"After figuring out how to open doors and operate the alien weapons and timing the guards of the prisoner floor on their rounds, the time finally came for them to make an attempt to escape. After stealing the keys to release them from their restraints and the chamber they were in, the explorers snuck out and raced to the departure bay, where their ship was held. Alarms went off, and guards rushed to the bay doors.

"Two of the explorers disabled the bay door control panel and used objects to obstruct the doors while the other explorers raced to their ship. After realizing that the bay door control panel was disabled, the aliens used their weapons to blast the doors open. By that time, the rest of the explorers had already boarded the ship, powered it on, lifted it off the bay floors, and began facing the exit.

"The other two sacrificed themselves by holding the aliens off as long as they could. They were recaptured. The explorers used their ship's cannons to blast the bay exit doors open to force the aliens away so they can depart the alien spaceship…and then they went… leaving two of their comrades behind. There was nothing they could do. They could either stay there and become slaves of the commander and die with them or leave them and tell their story.

"Months later, the surviving explorers made it back to Earth. They were evaluated and gave a complete report. After the evaluation, one of the explorers, who happened to be one of the founding scientists of our very facility, revealed that he had stolen some of the chips from the alien ship. His team immediately began studies on the chips.

"After months of trial and error, they began experimenting on animals. The scientists learned the mechanics of the microchips. They did some readjustments and upgrades and wanted human subjects. That's where you come in.

"After years of perfecting the microchip, the team realized the safest way to use them: splitting a chip into two pieces and inserting one side into a human brain and the other into an animal's. This will create a remote bond between the two.

"The DNA code makes bodies grow differently. That's why your animal counterparts don't age as fast as average animals. That's why you're able to share the five senses with them as well. That explains your telepathic links so you can hear each other's thoughts and such.

"The most exciting part is the transformations and special abilities. As you all have learned, you can transform and fuse with your animal partners, but there are other things about yourselves that you haven't learned yet. Your supervisors thought you weren't mature enough to teach you at the time. Maybe one day you'll learn on your own, or you can always just come back to the facility when you're ready.

"But the issue at hand is this: That alien ship that those explorers escaped from somehow found us. These creatures are space pirates. The commander lives to conquer and dominate. A lot of us will die. If they want prisoners, they will take. Worst-case scenario, they could destroy the whole planet.

"Each of you has your own superpower, thanks to these aliens, but now they're here. The good news is they have no idea we're prepared. Now that you have your feel of the outside world, the world needs you to use those powers to make sure it stays free.

"What do you say? You guys wanna show us what you've got?"

PREPARATIONS

MEANWHILE ON THE ALIEN MOTHER-ship, the creatures prepare for invasion, loading weapons. The commander, Lord Draegon, barks orders, which translates, "Team One, on land! Take anything of value and gather all the humans. Kill all who obstruct your mission. Team Two, fly around the perimeters. Destroy all that try to get in or out. Team Three, stand by for transport. Special teams, stand by for reinforcements."

Lord Draegon looks and points at the humans who are left with him.

"And I want you, humans, to go with Team One to make sure they're going in the right direction. You will lead us to the leaders of your planet so we can make an example of them. Your kind will tremble in fear of our power. If you try anything, my men will kill you."

———

MEANWHILE, BACK AT THE COMMAND Center, the president of the United States is on monitors all over the building, giving the country a speech.

"Try not to panic and stay inside your homes or in the safest place possible," he says.

In one of the rooms of the building, an agent is talking to the Nobodies on the man in the suit's phone. It's using the bluetooth on the vehicle's speakers.

"OK, we need to separate the team to cover ground. We need to be prepared to defend as much of the country as possible. We'll have jets on standby for transport in case adjustments are needed. There are military units posted all over the country. They are notified of your possible arrival. If and when you neutralize the threat in an area, you need to report back to us so you can be dispatched somewhere else to help."

The agent looks at one of the screens in the room.

"Uh-oh," he says.

On a live feed, a smaller vessel than the alien mothership is seen approaching the Command Center.

"OK, I need one of you over here right now! It's begun! The invasion has begun! Let's move!"

At that moment Angel volunteers.

"I'll go. Phoenix flies really fast. I'll be there in no time." She prepares to leave.

Cato leans toward her.

"A chance to show yourself what you can really do," he says. "Give 'em everything you've got. Don't hold back." He grabs her hand. "And be careful."

Angel smiles, then hugs and kisses Cato. She comes back with, "You be careful."

Diesel and Chaise lean in to add, "Good luck. Give 'em hell."

Angel nods. Phoenix descends to the vehicle's sunroof and morphs into a giant eagle. Angel climbs out of the sunroof and mounts Phoenix's feet. They ascend into the sky.

"Here are your destinations," the agent says to the rest of the team as he continues.

WORD FROM A BIRD

AS THE AGENT GIVES THE REST OF THE Nobodies orders, one of the alien ships approaches the Command Center. It's intimidating shadow slowly breaches the large campus of the building. Large pods begin to drop from the ship to the ground.

The Command Center's defense systems engage from the ground with heavy artillery such as .50 caliber machine guns and missile launchers. Soldiers gather behind the big guns to form a wall of defense with selected weapons of their own.

Out of the pods march the armed alien ground troops, standing about eight-feet-tall. They have dinosaur-like bodies with rough, scaly skin and sharp claws. They all march toward the Command Center and soon stop and stand by. One of the creatures in the command deck of the ship makes an announcement to the commanding officer. It translates, "Enemy weapons ahead!"

The commanding officer gives the order "Fire when ready! Obliterate!"

Immediately their ground troops and the ship opens fire at the Command Center's defenses. The human forces respond with an all-out assault of their own. Unfortunately, the machine guns only cause minor damage to the ship, and the missiles are diverted away from it. They explode in random places on the battlefield. The alien ground troops aren't as impermeable, but the Command Center's defenses are still not enough to deter the invaders.

The raiders' ship reaches the entrance of the building. The Command Center's forces are outmatched and will soon be outnumbered. Their men are being torn apart by the plunderers. They're surrounded with nowhere to go.

As the bad gets worse, the final pod drops from the ship and lands right in front of the facility. More enemy troops exit the pod, escorting one of the humans. Just as the human and alien troops all exit the pod, the sound of destruction is heard coming from the attackers' ship. The members of the final pod stop to look at their craft out of confusion. Random explosions occur throughout the hovering vessel. Then a high-pitched sound fades in.

An angelic birdlike figure flies into the fray. It destroys everything in its path with the sound of its voice. The intruders attempt to defend themselves, but the angel is too fast to zero in and land a shot on it. The swift movements, along with its high-pitched voice, helps dismantle the pirates in this fight. The Command Center now has a chance.

Finally, as the angelic figure zips through the battlefield, it begins to scream in a familiar tone. This brings all the raiders to their knees. They scream in pain as they drop their weapons and hold their heads tight, giving the Command Center's army a chance to regroup. One army man yells to the weakened adversaries as he points to his ears, "Special ear pro! From the pros, bitch!" Then he shoots them.

As the facility's troops regain their morale, the angelic creature lands by the commanding officer of the defenders. The half bird, half woman suggests to him, "You finish up down here, 'n' I'll finish up there."

The officer responds, "You got it! Wait. What should we call you?"

The half bird, half woman answers, "Harpy," and then dives back into the sky.

Harpy, the fused form of Angel and Phoenix, targets the opposers' ship above. She screams with all her breath. The sonic vibrations from her voice are so immense that she manages to force the enemy aircraft away from the Command Center. The alien technology on their shields protects the vessel from external damage but unfortunately not internally.

As the Command Center's soldiers gain control of the chaos on the ground, the foes' greatest weapon immediately targets Harpy. The ship fires at her but misses as Harpy dodges using the speed of her strong wings. The ship continues firing, but Harpy remains untouched as she maneuvers through the rain of fire.

As she remains evasive, Harpy suddenly finds an opening while facing the ship. She opens her mouth and screams again at the top of her lungs. The sonic vibrations echo throughout the entire ship, disabling a few weapons. Aboard the ship, one of the creatures reports, "Multiple weapons disabled."

The commander of the ship throws a tantrum and yells, "Take this pest out of the sky!"

Harpy, becoming arrogant, pauses for a second in face of the spacecraft and makes room for comedy.

"Oh, you haven't heard?" she jokes. "Here I thought everyone had heard!" She then dashes higher into the sky, singing "Surfin' Bird" as the invaders continue their attempt to strike her down.

Once she reaches a certain altitude, Harpy discovers the mothership of the invaders in outer space. Her eagle eyes give her telescope vision. She gets serious and dives back into battle as hard and as fast as she can. She takes a deep breath and begins humming a high-pitched tune. The sonic vibrations form an umbrella-like shield around Harpy. Once in range, the alien ship by the Command Center begins firing at her again. Harpy's shield deflects the assault of her enemies.

Finally, once close enough, Harpy uses the last of her breath to scream at her highest pitch. She spreads her wings to stop herself in her tracks. This turns her umbrella shield into a sonic bomb. A ball of echoing, vibrating destruction heads straight for the top of the alien spaceship at the speed of a rocket. Upon landing, Harpy's sonic bomb compromises the ship's shield and completely dismantles the entire ship by explosion.

The Command Center's forces finish eliminating the remaining threats from the alien ground troops. The human with them is retrieved, and Harpy lands near them as the members of the facility celebrate their victory. They invite her inside, where the agent who has given the Nobodies their assignments stands to welcome her.

ROUND TWO

MEANWHILE ON THE EXTRATERRESTRI-
al mothership, a crew member announces that one
of their units is no longer on radar. Draegon, still
cloaked, acknowledges with a wave of his hand.

Concurrently in New York City, US forces are in
a destructive battle with more of the raiding intruders. The citizens are in a panic, and the whole area is
chaotic. US forces are no match for the alien ship as it
bullies its way through the city's tall buildings.

Alien ground troops are all over the city, gather-
ing as many humans as they can, forcing them into
their pods. American fighter jets and attack helicop-
ters join the battle. They decide to use a jackham-
mer-like strategy on the enemy ship to break through
its force field.

Once they realize that the humans' strategy could work, the aliens use an electromagnetic pulse (EMP) to disable their enemy's aircraft. All aircraft in the vicinity begin to fall except theirs. The EMP terminates all power within a ten-mile radius. New York's defenses are now down.

With the US forces losing this battle, their rivals can take over the city with ease. Soldiers take cover and hide while the armed beasts continue capturing and killing. Once the pods fill with human hostages, they remotely lift off and return to the parent ship.

With the area almost completely seized by the plunderers, they begin to set up stations and stand guard. Suddenly, an unusual fighter jet enters the battle zone. Inside is the pilot, Diesel, and Torro. The pilot asks, "Where should we drop you?"

Diesel observes the enemy ship. "Let's focus on the big gun first," he suggests.

The pilot informs, "Weapons won't work. A report came in about it having a force field and an EMP. We may get hit with it if we get noticed."

Diesel rubs his chin while he thinks. "Hey, how high can this thing go?" he inquires.

The pilot looks to the side as an attempt to look back at him.

"What?" he asks out of confusion.

Diesel cradles Torro, who looks up at him. Diesel smirks.

"Let's touch the sky. Let's go!" he instructs.

At that moment, the only operational fighter jet in the vicinity is seen plunging into the upper atmosphere. Diesel removes his seat belt to prepare for his exit.

"Don't worry, the worst that can happen is me hurting for a minute. I'll be fine. Trust me," he assures the pilot.

The pilot continues gaining altitude. "Roger that! I guess that's why they call you Diesel, huh?"

Diesel stops the pilot. "I think this is good enough...and it's not Diesel. What you're about to see can only be done by Dozer."

Diesel presses the eject button, and he and Torro launch out of the jet. As the pilot descends to lower levels, he watches Diesel, holding Torro, transform into a giant minotaur.

"Oh...that's Dozer," he confirms.

Dozer dives horns first toward the roof of the alien aircraft. The speed of the descent makes Dozer a rocket from the sky. The ship begins firing at the minotaur as he closes in on his target.

Unfortunately for the occupants, it's too late. Dozer has enough momentum to disintegrate their ammunition. It doesn't even slow him down. Finally, he reaches forward with one hand, then cranks back the other with a tight fist.

"What happens when an unstoppable force meets an immovable object?" Dozer quizzes. "HOOAAAHH!!!" He yells on impact, landing fist first on one side of the spacecraft. The whole vessel tilts toward that side as it bows to Dozer's power. The ship's force field shatters, and a giant hole is now left where Dozer lands. He makes his entrance.

Not long after, the ship begins to explode in random areas. Dozer is inside, trampling through its walls in search of the power sources. All its occupants attempt to stop Dozer, but he's too powerful. Once he finds the engine room, Dozer begins the real demolition.

This causes a great explosion in the core of the shuttle, and it begins to plunge to the ground. All the foreign ground troops notice the crash landing about to happen. They all gravitate toward the landing area, leaving their hostages behind.

Dozer, like a wrecking ball, is inside the ship, destroying everything he can before the ship hits the ground. During his bulldozing, he accidentally finds the humans who have been transported there. Dozer orders them to take cover and hold on to something.

Once the opposers' spacecraft collides with the ground, the surviving US troops and citizens celebrate. Their greatest threat is neutralized. Once the alien ground troops arrive at the wreckage of their ship, thunderous quaking is heard coming from it. As the quaking gets closer, the creatures begin to brace themselves for whatever threat breaks through the walls of the vessel.

This gives the humans in the area time to regroup. They prepare themselves for another round as they gather weapons. Then out breaks Dozer! He leaps out and lands in a kneeling position with his fist in the ground. He looks up to discover he's surrounded by the enemy. At least one hundred of them are in sight.

"Well then!" Dozer speaks confidently with a snarl as he stands. The invaders look up at him as he stands about eleven feet tall. The creatures are about two feet shorter.

He cracks his neck and knuckles, then offers, "Round two?"

The raiders draw their weapons and fire on Dozer. His body is extremely resilient, however. The shots feel like a rain of pebbles to his skin. The minotaur stands there, welcoming the onslaught, as his body becomes covered in smoke. Once the attack ceases, Dozer's growls and heavy breathing are heard through the evaporating smoke.

"That stung," the minotaur claims.

His opponents become intimidated as he steps toward them. The whole army backs away with every step.

Dozer amplifies his tone. "Let's go!" he shouts as he becomes impatient and charges.

The once shaken enemy develops the courage to respond with a stampede toward the lonely warrior.

Dozer shows his power when he punches the first assailant head-on. The receiver is projected through the wall of his comrades. The minotaur continues to trample the rest as he swats, punches, rams, and slams each of the intruders. The creatures are no match for the powerhouse that is Dozer. Finally, he holds the arms of his last foe and headbutts him, ripping his arms off.

In that moment more US combat aircraft arrive to the battlefield. US ground troops have taken back their freedom. The human hostages exit their kidnappers' ship through the hole Dozer left behind. As they look around, they find the "big, scary monsters" lying on the ground motionless, and the even bigger one who has helped them escape is the only one standing as champion.

NEXT MISSION

MEANWHILE IN WASHINGTON, DC, THE
president of the United States and staff members are
all inside a safe place inside the White House. Their
security and a group of military men stand ready to
defend if necessary.

A thunderous sound is heard as explosions go
off outside the building. The look of fear reflects off
the staff members' faces. Tears fall, and prayers are
mumbled.

Outside is complete chaos. The monsters from
other worlds fight US troops for their hostile takeover.
The troops, however, are accompanied by a superpow-
ered werewolf and werecat. The werewolf is Chaise
and Coyote fused as one, and the werecat is the fusion

of Cato and Lynx. The werewolf's name is Feral, and the werecat is Sabre.

Feral and Sabre are about eight feet tall with sharp, bladelike claws. They also have claws bulging out of their knees and elbows. In addition, Feral has spikes on his knuckles, and Sabre has an arrowhead-shaped blade piercing out of the end of his tail. Feral and Sabre use their speed and their acrobatic martial arts skills to slice their way through the alien ground troops.

The invaders are no match for the teamwork of the animalized duo. They dash from every direction, dodging the alien attacks. Each enemy drops one by one at their hands. The alien ship, on the other hand, cannot be deterred. Feral looks up at it and attempts to jump toward the ship, but it shoots him down from his aerial pursuit.

Sabre analyzes the situation. "Gotta come up with a way to get to that ship," he thinks as he rushes to Feral's aid.

"You OK?" Sabre asks Feral.

Feral grunts as he recovers. "Yeah…goddamn, that hurts."

Sabre suggests, "The best thing for us to do right now is to remain on the ground and steer clear of their ship's fire until we come up with somethin'."

He asks, "Can you still fight?"

Feral responds out of anger as he growls, "Watch me!" He charges back into battle to finish off the enemy.

The ship reaches the White House, and several more pods eject out of it, surrounding the president's residence. One of the pods breaks through the roof and lands inside. Feral and Sabre rush toward the doors of the White House to help fight the oncoming enemies exiting their pods.

Not realizing the place has been infiltrated, the two can hear shots being fired inside the building as they fight off the foreign monsters by the front door. They stop to look at each other out of panic. Feral volunteers.

"Go! I'll take care of things out here." Sabre immediately breaks through the doors of the building to assist those inside.

Meanwhile, inside the safe place of the White House, the sound of gunfire, the roars of creatures, and the cries of wounded soldiers draw nearer. Anxiety fills the room as screams echo from the walls right next to the door to the safe place. Then suddenly heavy pounding arises at the door. Panic erupts in the room. The security people inside aim their weapons at the door, ready to open fire.

The pounding ceases. *Boom!* The door blasts open! Some of the men covering the door get knocked out from the blast. All the staff pile into a corner on the opposite end, screaming in panic. Two of the foreign monsters rush in, and the remaining armed men begin firing at them.

The aliens don't go down easily; however, their skin can take some damage. That gives them time to eliminate the resistance in the room before one of them falls. Then the surviving reptilian intruder announces in English, "I come for your leader...show your s—" The alien's sentence is interrupted while it falls to its knees, with Sabre standing behind it. Sabre holds a chunk of the enemy's spine in his bloody fist.

Sabre notices the panic in the room fading. He asks, "Is everyone OK?" as soldiers enter the room.

BACKUP

IMMEDIATELY AFTER, AN ERUPTION rumbles throughout the ground. Outside the White House stands a giant manlike, muscular, grizzly bear creature, about twelve feet tall. Its hair doesn't cover the torso area, and it carries a hammer that's just as huge as it is.

The giant presses a button on a device it's holding. The device sends a signal to instantly disable all weapons in the area, and the battle is muted. Feral then tells the commander of the US forces to order his troops to fall back and stay clear of the giant. The commander willingly complies.

As the troops fall back, Feral marches toward the giant fearlessly. "Big bitch," he says to himself.

The giant points at Feral and speaks in its language that translates, "Come, bow to your master."

Feral, unaware of what the giant has said, charges toward the beast, saying, "Oh, you talkin' shit?"

Once Feral is within its reach, the beast picks up his hammer and swings at Feral! The werewolf stops in his tracks and leans backward to dodge the wind-breaking attack. He touches the ground with one hand, then uses its force to push himself back into the fight.

The beast continues to swing as he roars "ARGH! ARGH! AAAAAARRRGGH!!!" but Feral is too fast and agile. He dodges the giant's ferocious blitz. Feral realizes that it's not going to be easy to get close enough to attack the beast. He decides to use a different approach by jumping backward to create space. He stretches his arms outward as his eyes and the spikes on his knuckles begin to glow.

The giant charges toward him. Feral then steps forward and clasps his fists together, with his knuckles facing his enemy. He unleashes a ball of multiple slashes toward the giant. The beast uses his massive hammer to shield itself, but Feral's ultimate attack slices through it.

The multiple slashes fade away, leaving the giant with a very short rod in its hand. Feral wonders, "What the hell was that hammer made of?"

The giant launches the rod at Feral, and the werewolf swipes it away. Without the giant's hammer, Feral's fight with it evens up a bit.

As the fight goes on, Sabre exits the White House, noticing his partner's battle. Just as he prepares to engage, the werecat senses movement behind him. Sabre quickly turns around to find nothing there. "Show yourself!" he commands with a snarl as his eyes dilate, enabling him to see even the slightest movement.

He notices a transparent, scorpion-like figure slowly approaching. Sabre shouts out of confusion, "What the!" as the figure attacks him.

Feral continues his fight with the giant by trying hand-to-hand combat. That puts him at a disadvantage because the giant is tough and overpowers Feral. The giant grabs him and effortlessly slams him to the ground.

In the background Sabre is spinning with the invisible creature's tail in his hand and releases it just as Feral is slammed to the ground. The giant cranks his fist back to finish him. In the nick of time, their fight is interrupted by the flying invisible creature, which knocks the giant off Feral.

The invisible creature loses its camouflage and shows itself as a giant scorpion-like reptile. Sabre shouts, "Stop playin' around, Feral! Let's finish this!" as he rushes toward their opponents.

Sabre jumps in the air and crosses his arms in front of his face, with his palms and claws facing outward. His eyes and claws begin to glow. He stretches his crossed arms upward and strikes down toward the enemy! He releases an X-shaped group of continuous slashes. They hit the two foes as they attempt to rise from the ground.

The giant grabs the reptile out of desperation and uses his ally as a shield. Sabre's ultimate attack slices through the giant's living shield, leaving the reptilian creature in pieces. The leftover slashes strike the giant and leaves great damage. The giant falls to its knees and lies on the ground immobilized.

Sabre lands next to Feral as he rises. Feral assures him, "I had 'em. You know that, right?"

Sabre looks back at the enemy ship releasing reinforcements and responds to Feral, "Sure you did. Now what are we gon' do about that?"

Suddenly the two notice an explosion coming from the alien ship, then more random blasts throughout. Feral wonders out loud, "What's goin' on up there?"

Sabre realizes what's happening and answers, "Backup," as the ship slowly begins to fall.

Feral asks, "From who?"

The internal destruction continues within the descending vessel as everyone on the ground attempts to evade it. Sabre grabs Feral to alert him.

"Now's our chance! Let's kick 'em while he's down!"

The duo prepares to unleash their ultimate attacks on the falling ship. This time concentrating for maximum exertion, they release greater projectiles with four times the power and durability. Their combined attack dismantles the enemy aircraft before it hits the ground.

Sabre looks at his hands and mentions, "I've always wanted to do that."

Feral agrees, "Right?"

Then a banging noise is heard coming from the ship wreckage. An object is seen ejecting from it, soaring into the sky.

The two Nobodies prepare for battle. Feral growls, "Boss level," as the object falls closer to them.

Suddenly Sabre relaxes and responds to Feral with a smirk, "Not exactly." The object lands near the pair and raises dust.

Out of the dust walks Dozer. He enters with a joke. "Ha! I just gave that bitch the D!"

Feral and Sabre celebrate. "All right!" Feral punches Dozer in the stomach and encourages, "I never thought I'd be happy to see you, but you proved me wrong today!"

Dozer smirks and replies, "There's a first time for everything."

Sabre interrupts, pointing at the sky, "Let's not celebrate too soon, guys. We got incoming."

Everyone observes the sky while a fleet of alien fighter jets approach them. Feral teases Sabre, "No way we can fight them while they're up there. What do we do now, O great wise one?"

Just as Feral asks his question, an answer is delivered with a high-pitched echo. It is followed by the sound of the destruction of the fighter jets. Harpy arrives, and she brings backup with her. An army of US fighter jets follows her closely as reinforcements.

With Harpy leading the way, they take down the enemy with ease and reclaim the sky. Once she's done, Harpy reunites with her team. As they celebrate, welcoming her in, Feral shouts, "Yooo! We are *live*!"

Harpy lands and alerts the group right away.

"Guys, we gotta move. They figured out a way to take the aliens down."

Sabre responds, "Sweet! But we need to make sure all the surviving aliens are taken care of first. Let's spread out 'n' help the military lock these fools up."

The team acts accordingly. They spread out, aid in search and seizure, and gather all foreign planetary creatures into one area. Once they finish, the team leaves the military to deal with the rest so they can move on to their next mission.

THE PLAN

BACK AT THE COMMAND CENTER, THE Nobodies regroup to find out how to finish off Earth's invaders. They walk inside one of the rooms for a briefing. Inside is a group of special operations soldiers highly skilled in missions such as the one they're about to face.

One of the soldiers, Master Sergeant Legend, jokes, "I'm fina' be the first black man in outer space! My name especially should go in the history books. I'm just sayin'."

At that time one of the scientists escorted by the aliens enters the room and calls, "OK! Attention, everyone!" All eyes turn to him. He continues, "This is how we defeat the enemy!" He holds up a computer microchip. "The information on this chip holds a virus that will immobilize all the aliens within a ten-mile radius of it! Here's the plan. First, we're going to need some of the escape pods that the aliens have in their ships. We're going to use those as our Trojan horse to get into their mothership in outer space."

As the scientist speaks, the team is seen boarding an escape pod with the two scientists who have been with the alien monsters. The pod lifts off into space.

The lead scientist continues, "Now these monsters are very intelligent, but they'll assume we're one of them. After all, none of our people know their tech, and you guys have driven enough of them back for them to believe it."

Upon arrival in the mothership's departure bay, the Nobodies, along with the two scientists, step out of their shuttle. Sabre reports, "We're in, standing by."

The lead scientist says, "We'll split into two teams. Alpha will go for the mainframe, which is in the command deck. Omega will go for the ship's power supply."

Another shuttle enters the departure bay. Feral is on the other side of the entrance doors, standing guard. He smells someone coming down the giant halls of the mothership, and he races to ambush them. Once the enemy is down, he reports, "All clear at the bay doors. Let's go, Omega." At that command, the group of soldiers in tactical space suits exit the shuttle and meet Feral at the doors.

The lead scientist says, "Alpha, escort my partner and me safely to the command deck. Once there, we'll insert this virus into the alien main computer. Once it's uploaded, all the mutants will fall."

Dozer and Harpy clear each path that Alpha takes, making the enemy troops drop, while Cato and the two scientists ride on the back of an evolved form of Lynx, a giant leopardlike cat. Once Alpha is close to the command deck, the lead scientist points and notifies, "That's the command deck. I need a distraction and cover."

Cato responds, "Dozer, you're up."

Dozer yells, "One distraction comin' right up!" as he rams through the command deck doors.

The lead scientist says, "Omega, you will plant explosive devices all throughout the engine room. Once the mission is over, you blow the place…if Alpha fails, you blow the place."

Feral and his team fight their way into the gigantic engine room. Once inside, the team spread out to plant their explosive devices in random positions throughout the room. They move as smoothly and quickly as possible. After what seems to be an easy assignment, the crew exits the room to return to the departure bay. Unfortunately, the Omega team is intercepted and surrounded by enemy soldiers.

Meanwhile, with the Alpha team, Dozer breaks through and clears the command deck of the mothership so that the scientists can operate the main computer. After clearing the room, Cato and Lynx fuse into Sabre. He and Harpy join Dozer to keep the room clear of enemies.

The scientists reach the main computer and insert their microchip into it. The virus downloads into the mainframe, and the scientist prepares to press the button of execution.

"Now once this virus is downloaded into the system, you guys," the lead scientist says, as he points at the Nobodies, "will have to be separated from your partners. Once activated, it may affect you too. So wait for my signal."

As the Nobodies continue fighting the foreign creatures, the downloading of the virus is 99 percent complete. The lead scientist notifies over their radio, "All right, Nobodies, it's time to separate."

Then Harpy changes to Angel and giant Phoenix, Dozer to Diesel and giant raging Torro, and Sabre to

Cato and giant Lynx. Feral, on the other hand, is fighting a large, hairless, doglike creature. It has a head and jaws large enough to bite Feral's upper body off. He's having a strenuous time with it while his team holds off the rest of the alien soldiers with their high-powered weapons. Feral responds while pinned against a wall, struggling to keep the doglike creature's mouth away from his head, "Argh! I can't right now! Kinda stuck in the middle of something!"

The lead scientist, who's just seconds away from pressing the button, insists, "We're ready, Feral! We need you to unfuse now! This window may not last much longer."

Feral grunts, "I need a minute!"

Cato jumps on Lynx's back and orders, "Lynx and I are coming! Hang on!"

He points at the scientists while ordering, "Angel, Diesel, stay and cover them!"

Angel and Diesel stand guard at the doors as Phoenix and Torro wreck the halls with oncoming alien bodies. The scientist urges, "We don't have time to wait! We must do this now!"

Then suddenly there's an explosion in the hallway near the command deck. In runs Angel as she carries a devolved Phoenix, and Diesel follows her from the other side of the hall to check on her. He asks, "She OK?" At that instant the lead scientist panics and presses the button of execution.

As Cato and Lynx race to aid Feral, they're stopped by more alien soldiers, but they end up collapsing to the floor. "No," Cato whispers to himself.

"Feral, are you there?" he calls as he and Lynx continue their pursuit. "Feral! Feraaaalll!"

A voice down the hall responds, "We're in here!"

Lynx turns to go down the hall. Around the corner the Omega team stands over Feral, who's lying on the floor, unconscious.

As he shakes his head at the matter, Legend says, "He almost had him." With the look of despair on his face, Cato asks the soldiers to help mount Feral on Lynx's back, and they all move to the departure bay.

SHOWDOWN

AS FERAL, CATO, LYNX, AND THE SOL-
diers travel back to their ship, Cato reports to the rest
of his team, "Guys, Feral is unconscious. We're taking him back to the escape ship. What's goin' on over
there?"

Angel responds, "Phoenix is down. We need backup right now!"

As soon as Angel transmits her message, another
intimidating explosion is heard. It rumbles through
the hallways of the mothership. Diesel rushes toward
the hallway, screaming, "Torro!"

Angel continues speaking on her earpiece. "Something
is still awake here, and we don't know what it is!"

Cato responds as he and Lynx hurry back to the
command deck, "We're on our way!"

Diesel returns inside the command deck, holding his little hamster Torro. Angel urges, "Hurry, Cato! Torro's down too now!"

After making that last report, the sound of giant footsteps is heard approaching. The voice of the owner of the footsteps speaks in English.

"Congratulations!" As the steps are heard reaching the doorway, in walks the commander of the ship. He's still cloaked by his clothing, and he continues, "You've accomplished what no other being has ever done."

Angel and Diesel hand their injured counterparts to the scientists and stand in front of them to protect them. The commander continues, "But this is where it all ends."

The second scientist questions out of disbelief, "How is this possible? You should be down like the rest of your army!"

Draegon responds, "I'm not like the rest of my army! Unlike them, I needed no scientific molecular reconstruction."

He continues as he takes off his cloak.

"I was born a conqueror!" And there standing in front of Angel, Diesel, and the two scientists is a fifteen-foot-tall beast of a dragon.

The dragon growls and leans forward to plant his hands on the floor. He claims, "Your so-called warriors have fallen. What will you do now?" Flame builds in his mouth.

Diesel turns to the second scientist and takes Torro back. He asks, "We can fuse now, right?" The scientist nods yes.

Angel takes Phoenix and orders the scientists, "When we fuse, you guys run for the departure bay. We'll cover you."

Then just as the dragon prepares to fire, he belches the flame right in the opposing group's faces and roars in agony. The group hits the deck, not realizing what's happening as the flame evaporates. Miraculously, on the back of their opponent is Sabre, with the blade from his elbow penetrating through Draegon's tough, scaly skin. Sabre dangles as he attempts to use his other elbow to penetrate Draegon's back for stability.

Unfortunately, the dragon's movement is too chaotic. He flaps his wings out of panic and tries to reach the area where the pain is coming from, but his arms can't touch it. So he uses his tail to swat Sabre away like a beach ball.

In the meantime, this gives Diesel and Angel time to recover from the ground and fuse with their partners. As Dozer stands, he boasts, "Now we're the so-called warriors you wanted to meet."

Then Harpy takes flight, and Dozer charges, saying, "Let's see what you've got!"

In that moment, the scientists flee. Sabre recovers from the wall he has been thrown into, and Harpy screams at the dragon until Dozer gets there. Draegon is defenseless to Harpy's sonic power. He kneels as if he is begging for mercy.

On arrival Dozer lands a superman punch to the dragon's face, knocking him backward. But using his wings to stabilize himself, Draegon regains his balance. Dozer continues his attack, but Draegon counters by quickly grabbing Dozer's arm and throwing him into Harpy. The two crash into the control system's equipment, leaving the spaceship uncontrollable.

In this instant Sabre pursues with his claws ready. Draegon fires his flame at him, but Sabre slides under it like in a game of baseball. The scorching blaze is almost too hot to bear, but it doesn't stop him on his pursuit. Sabre arrives directly in front of the dragon with his claws glowing and plants his feet firmly on the ground.

Draegon pauses in emitting his fiery breath and attempts to strike, but Sabre is already lifting off the ground. Sabre spins with a powerful slicing uppercut. A flashing slash emits from his left claw. Then he produces a downward slice of the same magnitude from his right.

The attack forces Draegon backward. He roars in pain. Sabre lands gracefully as the rest of the team recovers. He yells as the team regroups, "He can barely take on one of us! Let's show 'im it's not a game! Give 'im all we've got!"

As the dragon readies himself, Harpy takes flight again while Sabre and Dozer flank Draegon. This keeps them out of Harpy's targeted range. Harpy sings in a more powerful tone while concentrating her vibrations in a thinner stream. Draegon tries to resist, but the tune is too powerful. The floor crumbles, and Draegon sinks into it.

Then suddenly the singing stops, and the dragon looks up to find two enemies about to charge. Sabre jumps toward him on his right side, but the dragon punches him away with his left hand and swings his tail at Dozer instantaneously. Dismally for Draegon, Dozer catches his tail with both arms. Without hesitation, Dozer swings the dragon around, *slamming* him back into the weakened part of the floor he was in! The floor relents right after Dozer leaps to pounce on top of the dragon. This gives Dozer more momentum.

Once Draegon lands on the floor again, Dozer lands on his face fist first!

Dozer dismounts the apparently unconscious alien leader. Harpy, then Sabre enters the floor to follow up. Harpy says, "He's out! What did you do to 'im?"

Dozer shrugs. "You know me. I gave 'em tha' D."

As the group laughs at Dozer's joke, Draegon's mouth begins to fill with flames. Just as Sabre attempts to speak, Dozer is hit with a fireball! It explodes and throws him into a wall.

Draegon rises from the ground, only to be taken back to his knees by Harpy's sonic scream. Her vibrations are even more powerful than the last time. The dragon roars in anguish. His wings spread wide as the screaming persists. Draegon lifts himself off the ground to attempt flight but is denied by an X-shaped slice attack from Sabre. Harpy's singing ends on that note.

Sabre's ultimate attack leaves great wounds on their enemy and leaves him grounded but not finished. Draegon—scarred, bloody, and on his knees and elbows—lifts his head with a different colored glow in his mouth. He prepares his ultimate attack, but without warning, Dozer interrupts with a massive elbow drop to the conqueror's spine. The attack shakes the floor of the room with a small quake.

The glow evaporates from Draegon's mouth, and Dozer rolls over and pounds away at the finished opposer's face. After multiple explosive strikes, Dozer delivers the final blow to the face of their enemy to end the fight. Draegon lies there beaten and motionless. Dozer exhausts steam from his nostrils. "Bitch," he claims as Sabre and Harpy appear next to him.

Harpy asks, "Is it over this time?"

Sabre answers, "He's definitely had enough, but we should definitely take him with us out of here and lock him up. That's all you, D!" He slaps Dozer on the arm and takes off running toward the departure bay.

"Let's go!" Sabre shouts.

Dozer blows more steam from his nostrils and grabs the dragon's tail.

THE BAD NEWS

BOTH THE ALPHA AND OMEGA TEAMS regroup to a smaller space shuttle within the mothership. It's ready for takeoff inside the departure bay. On board the shuttle, Sabre sees the lead scientist, which reminds him about the reason for Feral's condition.

Sabre reforms back to Cato and Lynx and approaches the scientist aggressively.

"You! What were you thinking?" Cato growls as he pins the scientist against a wall. He shoves his forearm against the scientist's neck. "Look at what you did to him!" Cato points at Feral.

The scientist, in a state of consternation, answers, "I…I…I don't know. I'm sorry! I'm sorry! I panicked! There was an explosion, and people were running into the room! I didn't know what to think! I didn't know what else to do!"

Harpy notices the disturbance as she boards the shuttle. She reverts to Angel and Phoenix. Angel interrupts gently as she touches Cato's shoulder, "Cato."

Cato barely takes his eyes off his target, but Angel continues, "I'm sorry. We scared him into doing it. It was our fault. Don't blame him. We failed."

Cato eases the grip on the scientist, eventually releasing him. Then he walks away, punching the first wall within his reach.

"AAARRGH!!" Cato roars as he exits. Lynx follows him closely.

Meanwhile in the back of the shuttle, the special ops team is gathered. "We should do it to honor him," states Master Sergeant Legend to his team. "I think he'd like it. It was an honor to fight alongside him. Hopefully he gets a chance to hear about our new name."

He beats his chest with his fist. "Wolfpack on three!" he shouts. "One! Two! Three!"

The whole gang shouts together, "Wolfpack!"

Immediately after, Cato enters. His emotions remain written on his face. The self-proclaimed Wolfpack gives him their attention. Cato speaks.

"Thank you, all, for having his back. He probably would never show it, but he would be proud to have such a good team. I hope to see you around."

The shuttle enters Earth's atmosphere. Upon arrival at the Command Center, the crew is warmly welcomed. The alien commander, Draegon, is completely restrained and taken into custody, and Feral is taken to an emergency room.

Days later at the Command Center, Feral is lying unconscious on a bed. Outside the room stands Cato, watching him. Angel appears by Cato's side.

"How is he?" she asks.

Cato exhales saying, "The doctors say that he's fine physically, but none of them have a clue if he's ever gonna wake up."

"Cato!" a scientist calls with papers in his hand.

Cato and Angel walk toward him.

"I'm afraid I have some bad news," the scientist begins. "After scanning the microchip in Feral's brain, it seems that it's doing some serious rebooting."

"How is that bad news?" Cato inquires.

The scientist revises, "I'm sorry, I should've said reconfiguring. There's no information that reveals the separation of the two characters, Chaise and Coyote. I'm afraid Feral, whenever he wakes, will forever be

Feral. I'm sorry, Cato." The scientist walks away, leaving Angel and Cato in a frozen state of shock. Angel hugs him for comfort.

Suddenly the sound of glass breaking and a door slamming is heard coming from Feral's room. Cato and Angel rush to the area, where there's a path full of commotion. The couple examines Feral's room. The empty bed Feral has been lying in is protruding out of the window, sending broken glass on the floor. The door of the room is off its hinges and wide open.

The couple whisper to each other, "He's up!" Unexpectedly the sound of broken glass is heard again down the hall. They follow the path of the commotion. Angel wonders, "You think he's OK?"

Cato replies, "Knowing him, I can't say."

They arrive at a broken floor-to-ceiling window with a view of the outside. The couple looks down. They're five floors up, and Feral is nowhere in sight. With the winds from outside blowing in, Cato continues, "But he probably needs some time alone...hopefully he'll be back."

The couple continues to look out of the broken window. Angel responds to Cato, "I hope you're right."

A wolf's howl is heard in the distance.

ABOUT THE AUTHOR

RAFAEL HINES HAILS FROM SHREVEPORT, Louisiana, and is a bona fide comic book and anime aficionado. After serving four years in the US Army, including a tour in Afghanistan, Rafael turned his untamed imagination into the engrossing *Nobodies* universe. Inspired by late '90s and 2000s kids' shows, his debut novel *Nobodies: Domination* is the product of years of perseverance. Rafael aspires to captivate your imagination, just as his was captured during his formative years. There's more to come, so stay tuned!

Milton Keynes UK
Ingram Content Group UK Ltd.
UKHW021945101123
432363UK00004B/68

9 798822 926615